IF I COULD DRIVE A
FIRE TRUCK!

by Michael Teitelbaum
Illustrated by Uldis Klavins and Jeff Walker

Cartwheel
·B·O·O·K·S·®

SCHOLASTIC INC.
New York   Toronto   London   Auckland   Sydney
Mexico City   New Delhi   Hong Kong   Buenos Aires

ISBN-13: 978-0-439-31815-0
ISBN-10: 0-439-31815-7

TONKA® is a registered trademark of Hasbro, Inc.
Used with permission.
Copyright © 2001 Hasbro, Inc.
All rights reserved. Published by Scholastic Inc.
SCHOLASTIC, CARTWHEEL BOOKS, and associated logos are trademarks and/or registered trademarks of Scholastic Inc.

Library of Congress Cataloging-in-Publication Data available

12 11   12 13 14/0

Printed in the U.S.A.   40

First printing, November 2001

My name is Susan.
Today, I'm going to visit Grandma with my mom and dad.
It's a long drive, but I've got my favorite fire truck to play with.

WHEE-OOH! WHEE-OOH! WHEE-OOH!
A real fire truck races past us on its way to an emergency.
My dad moves our car out of the way and slows down.
Wow, look at that fire truck go!
What if *I* could drive a fire truck?

I would start my day in the fire station with all the other firefighters.

CLANG! CLANG! CLANG! CLANG! CLANG!

The alarm sounds. There's a fire in a house on Chestnut Street.

Everyone springs into action. Down the pole I slide!

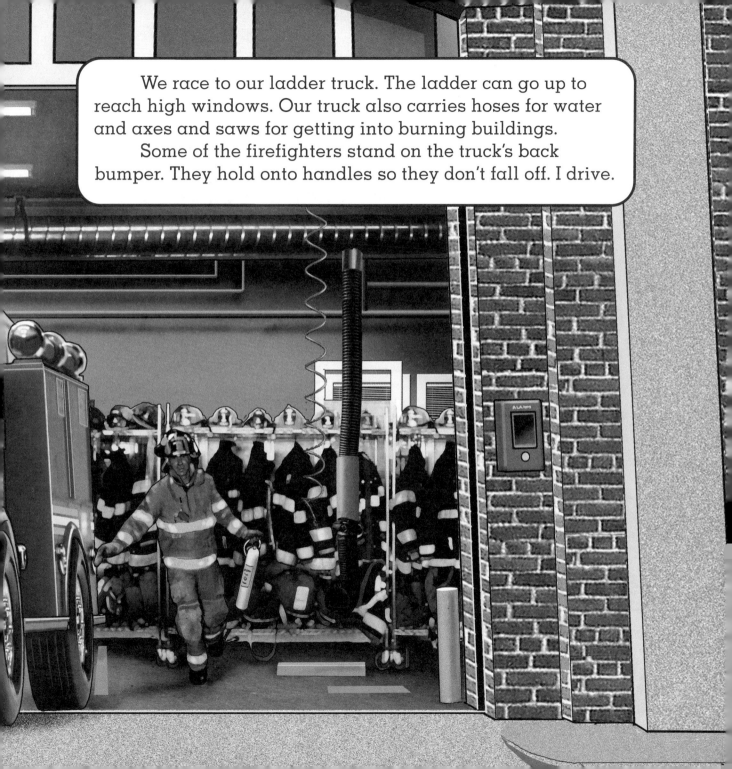

We race to our ladder truck. The ladder can go up to reach high windows. Our truck also carries hoses for water and axes and saws for getting into burning buildings.

Some of the firefighters stand on the truck's back bumper. They hold onto handles so they don't fall off. I drive.

I speed through the streets with my siren screaming. *WHEE-OOH! WHEE-OOH! WHEE-OOH!*
The other cars get out of my way. They know I'm racing to fight a fire, and every second counts!

In a few minutes, we arrive at the fire. The top floor of a house is burning. Flames and smoke pour from the windows.
The family who lives there has gotten out safely. Now it's up to us to save their home.

A police car screeches to a halt. The fire chief's truck is right behind it. Police officers keep the crowd safely away from the fire. The fire chief directs the firefighters as we battle the blaze.

Then an ambulance shows up to help any people who may be hurt.

Next, we raise our tall ladder all the way up to the windows on the top floor of the house.

I climb up the ladder. When I reach the nozzle at the top, I aim it at the flames.

WHOOSH!

A powerful stream of water pours from the nozzle.

Soon the flames are gone. The fire is out, and the building is saved.

The family thanks us for saving their home. Then the fire chief sends us back to the fire station.
Good job, firefighters!